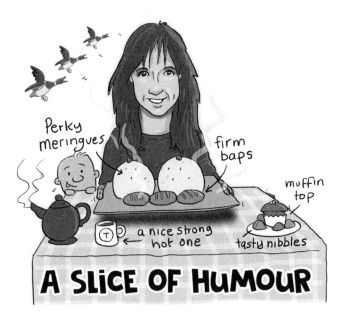

A SLICE OF HUMOUR

A collection of humorous poems by
Mrs Yorkshire the Baking Bard

Published by Red Lizard Books

Printed in the UK

Copyright © Carol Ellis 2018

About the author

Carol Ellis, who writes under the pen name Mrs Yorkshire the Baking Bard, was born in 1962 in Wakefield, West Yorkshire to Irish parents.

She has been married to Michael since 1985 and they have one daughter, Jessica, born in 1991. She has been living on the Isle of Man since 2007.

She is a performing poet, infamous for her stand up style of comedy in rhyme.

Her poetry has already featured in many local and national newspapers, in magazines and on Channel 5's daytime shows *The Wright Stuff* and *The Jeremy Vine Show.*

She writes observational poetry and her cleverly-crafted poems are both humorous, witty and will have you roaring with laughter.

She also writes poetry to touch the heart and has a talent for bringing very ordinary subjects to life through the rhythmical creation of beauty in words.

Acknowledgements

To my loving husband, Michael. I can always depend on you to support me in anything I do. You give the best advice and have shown me nothing but unconditional love and encouragement.

To my darling daughter, Jessica, the inspiration for my poem *The Empty Nest*. You make me proud every day. My life improved beyond measure the day you were first placed in my arms. You proved there is no bond like the one between mother and child.

To my wonderful mum, who gave me the gift of life. A lovely, nurturing mum from a long line of typical Irish mammies. You have devoted your life to your children and grandchildren and encouraged me to enjoy reading which awakened in me a love of language and writing. The poems I've written for you say it all.

To Chris Payne, who has helped, advised and guided me through the process of publishing. You have enabled me to realise my dream. You made me believe it could happen and made sure it did. I am so grateful for that.

To Graeme Hogg, a wonderfully talented and patient artist. Your illustrations surpassed all my expectations and have helped to bring my poetry to life. I can't thank you enough.

And last, but by no means least, to all my family and friends who have taken the time to read my poetry and watched me perform. Your unfailing support and kind words have given me the confidence to share my poetry.

Illustrated by Graeme Hogg

www.thewholehogg.carbonmade.com

Contents

A Catholic Education

If you've had the pleasure of being educated in a Catholic school, you'll definitely relate to this poem. If you weren't, you probably remember calling us names and resenting all those extra 'holy days of obligation' we had off school. After reading this you may feel a little guilty – which might just give you a better understanding of a Catholic education!

A Catholic Education

Even now I'm in my fifties
I remember well the sixties
Times were changing as a rule...
But then I went to Catholic school

At six we made our first confessions
Not too sure of our transgressions
I fear I must apologise
I told the priest a pack of lies

As part of holy education
Communion and our confirmation
I didn't mind them on the whole
A nice white dress and clean new soul

The bishop came and heard us sing
And later we all kissed his ring
He made us chant our rosaries
And watched us do it on our knees

In later years we held a dance
The priest not one take a chance
Made sure we didn't get too close
And left room for the Holy Ghost

At dinner we all said our grace
And then went on to stuff our face
But later when we all played sports
The boys were having impure thoughts

(Cont...)

On the bus with books and bibles
Other schools were our main rivals
Causing lots of aggravation
We got days of obligation

The seventies came to a close
I left unscathed though I
suppose
But some things just remain
in-built
I got an A-star grade in guilt

These days I'm not quite so naive
My mother's sad I don't 'believe'
Holy Mary mother o' God,
At least I'm not a bloomin' Prod!

A Yorkshire Valentine

*I wrote this poem in response to the gross
commercialisation of Valentine's Day.
I'm not saying I'm averse to romance
but as a down-to-earth Yorkshire lass I
certainly don't go in for splashing the cash
unnecessarily in order to impress others!*

A Yorkshire Valentine

Christmas is now over and they've paid
off all their debt
But February the 14th brings them out in
a cold sweat
They're off to flash the cash again and
frankly it's quite stupid
The question that I'd like to ask – just
who invented Cupid?

The shops are filled with heart shaped tat,
most of it quite cheesy
A teddy in a bright red thong can make
you feel quite queasy
The men are all so gullible, they're easily
coerced
They head off to Ann Summers where
'the customer comes first'

There's gadgets and appliances, designed
for every zone
He'd buy her a vibrator but he's sure she'd
only moan
He settles on a lacy basque complete with
black suspenders
She'd rather have a cup of tea and catch
up with Eastenders

(Cont...)

And once the day arrives let the hysteria commence
Splashing out on diamond rings, they've got more brass than sense
Proposals every hour, well it's all just too romanticised
But call me a traditionalist I find it too commercialised

Showing off their gifts and cards, they just can't wait to brag
Facebook full of sickly posts that make you want to gag
In days gone by a card was sent and always signed 'Anon'
All this tasteless showing off, it's just a massive con

Don't get me wrong I like true love, you couldn't call me fickle
I'm not averse to romance or a bit of slap and tickle
But being a good Yorkshire lass I'll give you some advice
Go shopping on the 15th when the chocolates are half price!

Bake Off Blues

I wrote this poem before the last series of The Great British Bake Off aired on BBC1 in 2016. Just after I wrote this there was great controversy when it was announced the programme would be re-made for Channel 4. Reading the final verse you may think I had a premonition! I'm well-known for my baking skills, my signature dish probably being my chocolate brownies with the Smarties on top. They were always a favourite with my daughter, her friends and her cousins when they were growing up so I couldn't help mentioning them in the poem!

Bake Off Blues

Bake Off's on the telly I thought that I'd
apply
With baps like mine I'm sure it won't be
hard to qualify
I've got lots of experience, I think I could
compete
My hubby says my plum delight is very
moist and sweet

He likes to get my cupcakes out he thinks
they're quite an eyeful
He's very kind he says that I remind him
of a trifle
I thought it was a compliment, but now
I'm feeling rotten
Because he says I'm fruity with a great
big spongy bottom

A Yorkshire tart is popular I go down
well at parties
I'm known bring my brownies out, the
ones topped off with Smarties
I'm partial to a cream horn, I prefer a
nice big whopper
You should see the size of my meringues
they'd make a great showstopper

(Cont...)

The ladies love Paul Hollywood, his smile
is quite disarming
I think his perfect dough balls make him
really rather charming
He's skilled with both machine and hand,
it's all in the wrist action
Although I've tried his spotted dick and
don't see the attraction

I just adore both Mel and Sue, the queens
of smutty talk
We'd joke about popped cherries and
then laugh about pulled pork
For us to share the baking tent would
surely be quite brave
And poor old Mary Whitehouse would
be spinning in her grave

I do like Mary Berry but I don't think
that she'd risk it
My swearing and my saucy jokes would
likely take the biscuit
My language surely won't be fitting for
the BBC
They wouldn't want a lady with a potty
mouth like me

I think I'm much more suited to a slot on
Channel 4
I could be the next Nigella, I'd be known
as 'The Cake Whore'
I'll get onto it straight away and write my
application
I'm ready to unleash my Cherry
Bakewells on the nation

Carol for Christmas

I actually enjoy Christmas once it's arrived but, like many people, I find a lot of the preparation and all that goes with it very tiresome. Please enjoy a lighthearted look at the festive season.

Carol for Christmas

Christmas is coming, we're all getting fat,
it's costing a fortune too
We're constantly spending, it's just
neverending
I'm brassic between me and you

Trawling the shops for a bargain, I'd
rather be out having fun
To save myself time, I'll be shopping
online
But the courier plays knock and run

They're queuing for hours to see Santa,
he's out the back having a fag
Then an awful brat said that the elves are
all dead
And the fairy's a fella in drag

Don't mention the office party, the
behaviour's most certainly risky
They fill up their glasses and make
awkward passes
And everyone's feeling quite frisky

Visiting family at Christmas, the travel
arrangements are made
The trains are quite crammed and the
roads are all jammed
And of course all the flights are delayed

(Cont...)

The telly's not like in the old days, we all
settled down with high hopes
We watched Morecambe and Wise and
then Stars in Their Eyes
Now it's death and despair in the soaps

The X Factor's ruined our Christmas,
they'll likely achieve number one
We loved Wizzard and Slade, even
Wham! and Band Aid
What a pity those days are all gone

He's bought me a G-string for Christmas,
he hopes to arouse my desire
He's now on the brandy and getting quite
randy
He's roasting his nuts by the fire

Santa's the true star of Christmas he's got
lots of presents to give
As he travels the miles, he's all laughter
and smiles
'Cos he knows where the naughty girls
live

There's still loads of leftover turkey, I'm
making a bubble and squeak
I'm not really chuffed 'cos we're all pretty
stuffed
And it's bloomin' new year in a week!

Costa Fortune

As a down-to-earth Yorkshire lass I'm not one to follow the crowd, especially if it means wasting my well-earned cash. I try, wherever possible, to support the local small shops in my nearest town of Ramsey here on the Isle of Man. When they opened up a second Costa coffee shop in Ramsey I felt compelled to pen this poem which also reflects on how times and attitudes have changed over the years.

Costa Fortune

They've opened up a Costa in the
Mooragh Park of late
We'll soon have one in every major city at
this rate
There was a time you'd never eat your
dinner from your lap
You boiled the kettle for a cuppa, got your
water from a tap

What happened to 'Freedom to flourish'
and 'Thanx for choosing Manx'?
We've got Pizza Hut and Starbucks and
McDonald's like the Yanks
Multinationals everywhere, there's one in
every acre
From the butcher to the baker to the
candlestick maker

Once your mother cooked your food, you
ate it at the table
Sarnies made on proper bread and not
some fancy bagel
A supper from the chippy was reserved
for special holidays
A take-away three times a week is just
expected nowadays

(Cont...)

Kids played out in raggy clothes and
came home tired and mucky
No designer trainers, yet we thought
ourselves quite lucky
We didn't have computer games, were
thrilled to have a spacehopper
Were happy with a 10p mix, delighted
with a gob stopper

Ladies painted their own nails with
polish from the shop
Now they're paying someone else at
thirty quid a pop
Hiring personal trainers to ensure that
they are fit
Make sure to take a selfie in their trendy
gym outfit

Let's all go on a city break, a weekend at
a health spa
Get botox in our lunch hour and then
live just like a film star
All they seem to care about is instant
gratification
Drink gallons of Prosecco as a form of
medication

(Cont...)

There seems to me to be an urgent need
to waste your brass
It's hard to understand when you're a
good old fashioned lass
I don't need to splash the cash in order to
have fun
And being married to a Yorkshireman
I'm very cheap to run!

A small sherry at Christmas for a lady
was a treat
Now they're drinking pints and falling
over in the street
Everything they have on show – no such
thing as censorship
Drink as much as any man, wake up next
morning in a skip

Remember when a man was happy
tinkering in his shed?
Now they're wearing man bags, have
their eyebrows waxed instead
There's a very strange obsession with the
'back, sack and crack'
Proper men with hairy chests should
make a real comeback

I wish that folk would cherish, the simple
things in life
I'm happy baking buns and being a
mother and a wife
To some folk this seems rather strange
they're often quite perplexed
They'll be telling me to ditch my apron –
Eeee whatever next?!

Eurovision

Very tongue in cheek, here's a little dig at the Eurovision Song Contest. We all know about block voting and the politicisation of the contest. In 2017 I wrote this poem just after it had been announced that the UK had voted to leave the EU. Read it and weep, music fans.

NIL POINTS!

GB

Eurovision

If you're into cheesy kitsch, are partial to
drag queens
Enjoy a bit of yodelling, gigantic wind
machines
It's time to 'make your mind up', it's the
campest show on earth
I'd rather pass a gallstone or experience
childbirth

This festival we once embraced with
much hullabaloo
But that was in the days of Abba singing
'Waterloo'
With Terry Wogan's gentle wit – it wasn't
quite so brash
Before it got political, turned into
Eurotrash

Block voting is expected in the interests
of peace
So Norway vote for Sweden and then
Cyprus vote for Greece
My money's on the Scandics, Slavics,
former Soviets
Before the dodgy voting I advise you
place your bets

(Cont...)

They hate us 'cos of Brexit so I don't
fancy our chances
'Nil points' is all we can expect under the
circumstances
Next year I have a cunning plan
involving sabotage
We'll throw a spanner in the works and
send Nigel Farage

Halloween

Oh dear, why do we have to copy everything the Americans do? In my day we didn't really celebrate Halloween. Our mums scooped out a swede and stuck a candle inside and off we went to hang out with our mates for the night, dripping wax on the back step as we went. No fancy costumes and parties for us.

Halloween

In times gone by we didn't even mention
Halloween
In those days only 'penny for the guy'
was on the scene
Bombarded by the Yanks it seems the
Brits have been persuaded
Commercialism rules the day, our
culture's been invaded

Nineties kids were happy with a bin liner
to wear
It's now designer fancy dress, I really do
despair
We spend all year reminding kids 'now
don't talk to a stranger'
Then send them out to knock on doors
and disregard the danger

We spend a fortune buying treats and
stash them in a drawer
Just in case the little blighters knock
upon the door
Held to ransom by a small machete
wielding brat
We daren't say no in case they chuck a
firework at the cat

(Cont...)

They take off to a neighbourhood where
folk are well to do
There'll be pound coins there a-plenty
and they'll make a bob or two
Not for them the penny chew or cheap
treats bought from Lidl
Frosted home made cupcakes with a
ghoul stuck in the middle

And when the night is over and they've
counted up their haul
They could open up a corner shop, the
size of their windfall
The parents are no better – they join in
the competition
Dressing up like ghosts and ghouls,
devoid of inhibition

A lass can dress just like a slut – a sexy
cat or witch
Knowing that her so called friends will
not have grounds to bitch
A dad dressed like a skeleton makes all
the kids uneasy
A fat man in a lycra suit can make you
feel quite queasy

(Cont...)

Horror films on every channel, shown
year after year
Even all our favourite shows are
peddling death and fear
Halloween themed episodes and
Strictly's not immune
They're wearing ghoulish costumes
dancing to a spooky tune

Now you might think that I'm inclined
to be a little mardy*
Just because I won't partake and think
them all foolhardy
They'll be itching from the face paint and
they'll soon look pretty naff
When they've all got dermatitis I'll be
having the last laugh!

(mardy, Yorkshire slang – definition:
miserable)*

Love in the Fast Lane

This poem was inspired by my husband's love of restoring classic motorcycles. As motorcycles age, all kinds of problems arise, and this made me realise that wives are really not much different than their beloved motorcycles to the biker!

Love in the Fast Lane

Back in his youth he was born to be wild
She was quite fast and was perfectly
styled
Her hefty front end was a sight to behold
Her rear end was soft but quite wobbly
I'm told

He got his leg over and rode her at last
He cranked her right over, went hard and
went fast
She did respond well to her motorbike
rider
The throb of his engine went right up
inside her

But as the years passed well it all went
awry
The cost to maintain her was getting
quite high
She needed more oil and complained she
was shattered
She started to whine and she constantly
chattered

(Cont ...)

It has to be said that her gear box was flagging
She started to leak and her front forks were sagging
Her clutch was now worn, she'd an old droopy seat
She tended to drip and would then overheat

His helmet's quite sweaty and she's not impressed
His big end has gone and he's way past his best
She sits by the fire, her cheeks are quite red
She's warming his supper while he's in the shed

She started to fail and then sadly she died
The hearse took her off on that last gloomy ride
For all their misfortunes he misses his spouse
But at least he can now bring his bike in the house!

Photoshopped

*Admit it, how many of you photoshop your
photos before you put them on Facebook?
So many people take selfies, then use
software like Photoshop to smooth out the
blemishes before putting the photos on
Facebook. I have to say I don't, but this is
partly because I'm not tech savvy enough
to be able to master it and mostly because
I'd hate someone to meet me in the street
and not recognise me if they hadn't seen
me in person for a while. I know some
people who do this all the time (they shall,
of course, remain nameless) but they
inspired me to write this poem!*

Photoshopped

I met up with a long lost friend, it sure
had been a while
I'd found her via Facebook and I'd
checked out her profile
She'd worn quite well, was looking great
– or so I had believed
But when I met her in the flesh I found I'd
been deceived

We're not supposed to mention it, the
subject is taboo
She was nothing like her profile pic
between both me and you
She'd used a fancy filter in an effort to
look pretty
But to tell the truth her edit skills were
really rather shitty

The web is full of phony folk they're
slaves to Photoshop
Painting on their six packs, every photo
cropped and chopped
Shiny foreheads mostly free from
wrinkles or a frown
Fake blusher makes them look like some
extreme makeover clown

(Cont...)

Dazzling artificial smiles designed to
mesmerise
Like Pokemons on steroids with
humungous glowing eyes
I didn't know that they had found a cure
for cellulite
Removing imperfections, not a lump or
bump in sight

The news reports have told us that the
lady's disappeared
The cops released her photo I'm afraid
the worst is feared
Her husband's quite distraught – I don't
believe they'll find his wife
On her Facebook she's Beyonce but
Chewbacca in real life!

Rain

*Let's face it, in the British Isles we
generally get on average nine months of
winter/autumn weather and three months
of 'summer'. It's a great disappointment
when the months without an 'r' in them
fail to reach 70 degrees and our car boot
sales and barbeques are ruined by wind,
gales and rain!*

Rain

It's raining, it's pouring, it's just getting
boring
It's now July but no blue sky
Let's have some global warming

Men like giant toddlers wear t-shirts and
long shorts
Ladies dressed in tiny tops with not
much for support
Let's all remove our bedsocks and put
away the vest
I'll put my sexy nightie on and not feel so
oppressed

I thought I felt the sun last week,
warming my old bones
Alas it was a false alarm and only my
hormones
I'm sick of these excuses, they blame it
on the jet stream
I want to go down to the park and sit
there eating ice cream

At Glastonbury they drink champagne
and frolic in the mud
They wear designer wellies, in case there
is a flood
Glamping in a fancy yurt – it's all a great
expense
But dysentery is not much fun, they've
got more brass than sense

(Cont...)

Rain stops play at Wimbledon, they're
really not impressed
And now Cliff Richard's singing and he's
asking for requests
He's done 'Congratulations' and now he's
singing 'Move It'
He did it for the ball boys – although I
couldn't prove it

I'm not beach body ready I'll have to
wear a kaftan
I resemble an Albino and I need to get a
spray tan
And now my legs need waxing, I'll have
to paint my toenails
I've booked a full bikini wax – I'll spare
you of the details

I'm going to a barbeque, I'll take some
cans of Stella
There's burgers and some sausages served
up with salmonella
But suddenly a thunderstorm the sky's
turned grey and dark
I'm bloody sick of all this rain I'm off to
build an ark!

Starbucks Saga

By now you'll have noticed I'm not one to follow the latest trends or waste my well-earned brass. When our capital city, Douglas, acquired a Starbucks coffee shop I was inspired to write this poem. Again, very tongue in cheek and no offence meant.

Starbucks Saga

Starbucks is coming to Douglas to the
thrill of the posh coffee drinker
The punters of course will be right out in
force
To fall for it hook, line and sinker

But don't tell me to pay them a visit 'cos I
won't be conned by the hype
This shrewd northern lass will not part
with her brass
To pander to them and their type

Most days you can find yummy mummies
discussing some parenting fad
They drink cappuccino and sip
frappuccino
And flirt with the stay at home dad

Ladies that lunch after yoga, desperate to
turn back the clock
With a face full of plastic, they surely look
drastic
To the cosmetic surgeon they flock

Like an old car in the scrapyard the
bodywork's not up to much
They've set their sights on new headlights
And a lovely designer new clutch

(Cont...)

You can keep your fancy barista I'll stick
to my nice Yorkshire Tea
They're charging the max and avoiding
their tax
But they won't get a penny from me

The Come Over

This is a very affectionate poem written about my experience of moving from God's own county (Yorkshire) to the Isle of Man. Each place has its own little customs and curiosities and the Isle of Man is no different. I've been welcomed with open arms and open hearts by the Manx people and feel very lucky indeed to live in such a beautiful place. Of course, should I ever complain, the Manx have a saying – 'there's a boat in the morning'!

The Come Over

One rainy day back at the end of March
2007
We packed up all our clobber and we
landed in this heaven
From God's own county we set sail to
reach the Isle of Man
Our worldly goods and all we had
packed in a big white van

A land without a Debenhams, no Asda
or Ikea
Why there's only Tesco here I've really
no idea
No Morrisons or Aldi not a Primark will
you find
Ask directions to the pound shop and
they'll think you've lost your mind

But soon they opened up a Dealz with tat
and shite a-plenty
We weren't too pleased to find out that
the charge was £1.20
We heard that down in Douglas, the
streets were paved with gold
But only up in Athol Street* is that the
case I'm told

(Athol Street, the financial centre of
Douglas)*

(Cont...)

We ventured out to have our snap I
fancied something hot
Chip butty on a teacake, but that's not
what I got
A plate of chips but by the 'eck you really
won't believe it
Currants in my teacake – well I had to
bloody leave it

'The plain ones are called baps', said the
waitress rather shaken
'Oh no' I said, 'that can't be right, I think
that you're mistaken
In Yorkshire baps are what we call our
boobies if you please
And I'd love to see you try to eat your
flamin' chips off these!'

We soon discovered to our cost the
weather is unruly
Don't hang your washing on the line if it
should 'blow a hoolie'
Scattered in the garden, and in the field
afar
I saw a sheep in knickers and lovely
matching bra

They told us Maughold was quite posh,
the God squad wouldn't like
Their hymns and service ruined by a
revving motorbike
No coloured lights at Christmas, 'oh
yessir only white'
I had to keep my bush trimmed lest the
vicar had a fright

(Cont...)

We settled in, and made our mark, my
baking was a hit
I wowed them with my muffins and they
loved my strawberry split
A Yorkshire tart was new to them, they
couldn't wait to try it
And when I got my cupcakes out there
damn near was a riot

Nine years have passed we love the folk
and all their funny ways
Bikers rule the island once a year for
fourteen days
Tax haven or the r.a.t. are words that
won't be spoken
Greeting fairies on the bridge, a rule that
can't be broken

Rolling hills, coastal walks and cats
without their tails
Being stuck without a boat or plane
because of winter gales
Eating kippers, queenies, oh and gravy,
chips and cheese
Singing 'Ellan Vannin' by our very own
Bee Gees

We love the flag with its three legs, just
like that Jake the Peg
But now we know what he was up to with
his extra leg
Don't mock the Manx or moan about
them, here's a word of warning
'Cos if you do they'll tell you 'There's a
boat in the morning!'

Sex Through the Ages

When we're not talking about the weather we do like to talk about sex and even, on occasion, indulge in it. This poem reflects on the different experiences of sex at each stage of life.

Sex Through the Ages

Back in the day when they first found
true love she was eighteen and he was
just twenty
He grabbed her at random, made love
with abandon
Their love life was varied and plenty

They're now middle-aged and to tell
you the truth their sex life has certainly
dwindled
But with some inclination to seek
inspiration
There's hope that it could be rekindled

They decided to try a new hobby, signed
up with a group of bell ringers
But they're all going to hell – and the
vicar as well
As it turns out they're actually swingers

They were seen heading out every
evening, they'd seemingly taken up
jogging
But I have to report, they're appearing in
court
It transpires that they've really been
dogging

(Cont...)

The story unfolded from bad to worse it's
such an unfortunate caper
They tried to be nameless but now they're
both famous
They've made the front page of the paper

She still has the bloom of youth in her
cheeks and the cheek of youth in her
bloomers
Although he's quite old, he's still active
I'm told
And the subject of neighbourhood
rumours

They say it's not true that the fire's out,
just 'cos there's snow on the roof top
His hair's turning white and his trousers
are tight
There's a balcony over his toy shop

She had a few friends round one evening,
and hosted an Ann Summers party
And much to his joy, she acquired a sex
toy
And an outfit exceedingly tarty

She bought a new see-through nightie,
looked good in it from every angle
She did try her best – but she left on her
vest
And it just caused his manhood to
dangle

(Cont...)

They're having a ball in their eighties,
she still finds it hard to resist him
When she feels the need, he's not up to
the deed
There's Viagra of course to assist him!

The TT Races

For two weeks at the end of May/ beginning of June, our small island, with an average population of 83,000 people, is invaded by hoardes of bikers from all over the world, many of whom return year after year to worship on the hallowed ground of the TT track. On average over 40,000 people visit the island to watch the races which are held on public roads and reach speeds of over 200 mph! Hold onto your helmets and enjoy this poem. Whether you follow motorsport or not, this will tell you everything you need to know about the wonderful TT Races!

The TT Races

The riders are eagerly waiting, they've
loaded the bikes with their gear
They've packed their cases for the TT
Races
For the best fourteen days of the year

They're stung by the Steam Packet price
hike, but consider it money well spent
They've really mucked up, the hotels are
booked up
So they're spending two weeks in a tent

They take a trip up to the grandstand, to
chat with McGuinness and Dunlop
And as they pass by, have a cuppa with
Guy
And a good rummage round in his
workshop

You can see that the girls are excited, at
the sight of the men dressed in leather
These ladies are tameless and utterly
shameless
And strain to keep their legs together

A lass takes a trip to the beer tent, she'll
find true romance in there maybe
But soon she conceives and the lad ups
and leaves
And she's left with her own TT baby

(Cont...)

The rides at the fair are quite costly, they
need to approach them with caution
They'll have to think twice when they tell
them the price
It's a definite form of extortion

The roads are increasingly busy, when
travelling to work every day
Then some continental who's totally
mental
Is riding his bike the wrong way

They set off from work in the evening
they all leave the office at five
They do tend to whine when they get
home at nine
'Cos it should be a five minute drive

For the sake of the riders and tourists, we
hope that the weather is sunny
And that those who attend are quite
happy to spend
To ensure that we make lots of money

It's the best time of year on the island, the
cynics had better take warning
If they want to complain, there's no need
to remain
There's an overpriced boat in the
morning!

They're Bringing Back Blind Date

How times have changed since the 1980s when the original Blind Date TV show was aired. Hosted by Cilla Black, it ran from 1985 to 2003 with a special one-off edition in 2013 to celebrate Cilla's 50 year career in the entertainment industry. Sadly, Cilla died in 2015 but the show made a comeback in 2017 hosted by her good friend, Paul O'Grady. Paul was a very good personal friend of Cilla's and has enjoyed a long and successful career, including, for a time, as a lady called Lily Savage!

They're Bringing Back Blind Date!

A bloke was searching on the net for love
the other night
She looked like Kim Kardashian, so
quickly he swiped right
'Petite, good sense of humour' well she'd
make the perfect wife
He met her for a date but she was Gollum
in real life

Before the days of Tinder things were
better I believe
No Photoshop or filters made it harder to
deceive
Those days are dead and gone with such
technology emerging
It was so long ago that even Lily was a
virgin

He was getting quite disheartened in his
search to find a spouse
Of course it didn't help that he would
rarely leave the house
But things are looking up, I think he
might just find a mate
He's going on a game show 'cos they're
bringing back *Blind Date*

(Cont...)

They've had a total revamp to adopt more modern ways
Transexuals, bisexuals and lesbians and gays
And mindful of diversity the host is Paul O'Grady
But that's OK because we've heard he used to be a lady

The lad had choice of suitors they were called one, two and three
There wasn't much to choose from though between both you and me
He chose a nice, sweet lass, she had a certain emanation
Alas that strange aroma was the smell of desperation

Paul was heard to mention 'times are hard and friends are few'
And Channel 5 have said they're keen to save a bob or two
No Maldives or exotic breaks where folk can get a tan
The only island they'll be on is called the Isle of Man

They set off on the ferry hoping that they'd find romance
She'd packed a see-through nightie, leaving not a thing to chance
She donned her sexy garment – the poor lass did try her best
But she was bloomin' freezin' and she had wear her vest

(Cont...)

When they returned to tell the tale it
hadn't gone to plan
They'd heard some creaking noises lying
in their caravan
Was that a ghostly presence or a faulty
thermostat?
'Surprise, Surprise' it's Cilla in a great big
wedding hat!

A Visit to the Dentist

We all have our own horror stories to tell about our experiences in the dreaded dentist's chair. After many years I've actually found a great dentist and made friends with him. I even bring my dentist and his staff some cake when I have an appointment! Next time you visit the dentist, read this poem before you go, as it might just make you laugh. Take a copy with you and pin it to the ceiling above the chair!

A Visit to the Dentist

When I was young I didn't brush and
floss my teeth each day
I skipped most of my check ups too I'm
quite ashamed to say
I was partial to a penny chew, no stranger
to a gobstopper
I even broke a tooth when bouncing
round upon a spacehopper

My mouth is full of fillings and a fair few
teeth are missing
Although it's never hindered me, I'm
pretty good at kissing
Eating crusty bread these days can prove
quite problematic
The thought of chewing toffees now is
really quite traumatic

I've known a good few dentists they were
all inclined to frown
They tutted and they muttered and gave
me a dressing down
But now I've found a dentist who is not
prepared to judge
Especially as I bring cake, his favourite –
chocolate fudge

(Cont...)

He's an expert in his field displaying skill
and great technique
He has a lovely turn of phrase – most
likely 'cos he's Greek
As I lay back into the chair I wonder what
he'll find
I must confess I'm nervous as he moves in
from behind

I've cleaned and flossed and even used an
interdental brush
To save any embarrassment I've washed
around my mush
No bogies up my nostrils, no stray hairs
upon my chin
Now I'm ready for inspection and to see
what lies within

He's found a hole and so he tells me that I
need a filling
He'll have to do an x-ray first before he
starts the drilling
The nurse brings a lead apron – for
protection I assume
Although it's disconcerting when they leg
it from the room!

He numbs me up, prepares his tools – a
burr, a probe, a torque wrench
And lays them out across my chest which
now looks like a workbench
And when the deed is done I feel an
urgent need to washout
He's the only bloke you'll ever find who'll
tell a lass to spit out

(Cont...)

I miss the bowl completely and it lands
upon the floor
In my haste to leave I slip and slide right
through the door
I've chipped a tooth, I felt it lodging
somewhere in my cheek
They've booked me an appointment the
same time again next week!

The Village Fete

*Our annual 'Parish Day' (otherwise
known as a village fete) held in the lovely
village I now call home is reminiscent of
days gone by. Knobbly knees and fancy
dress competitions, the crowning of the
Parish Queen, competitive sports in the
field, including the egg and spoon race,
the wheelbarrow race and the tug-of-war
and afternoon tea in the village hall. The
event brings the whole community of all
ages together. Just imagine though if we
had to abide by those pesky EU rules on
health and safety and inclusivity. It would
more than likely be a very different story
indeed...*

The Village Fete

We were holding a fete on the village
green it's traditional every July
We were having great fun and we even
had sun
Then the man from the council dropped
by

The kids from the school kicked off
singing and we started to cheer and
applause
As they sang the first piece he advised
them to cease –
They were breaching the copyright laws

Then a girl in a fetching white garment
stepped forward to crown the new queen
But he moved in to stop her, and said 'it's
not proper –
That child should be wearing sunscreen'

Bonny babies were scrapped from
the programme on advice from some
paediatricians
He wasn't best pleased with the knobbly
knees
And resolved to ban all competitions

(Cont ...)

Then up to the field for the races, he
thought it was all rather strange
He agreed with good grace to the egg and
spoon race
Just as long as the eggs were free range

The Jack and Jill race was updated, to
abide by the rules of inclusion
Then a worthy contender said he was
transgender
To add to the fuss and confusion

The gluten-free cakes were most welcome
and he couldn't complain about hygiene
But the tea was now made and it wasn't
Fairtrade
And the drinks were all loaded with
caffeine

The go-karts were subject to speed tests
overlooked by that meddlesome fella
But despite our posh loo, there was no
barbeque
Over fears that we'd catch salmonella

But we're not in the UK or Europe and the
Manx won't be taken for fools
We don't care about Brexit, so quickly he
legs it
To hell with his daft EU rules

Snowmaggedon

Oh dear, it seems we can't cope with extreme weather these days. At the slightest dusting of snow, drivers abandon their cars, the buses are called in, the trains cease to run (apparently this can be caused by the 'wrong kind of snow'), schools are closed and adults take 'snow days' bringing the country to a virtual halt. How ever did we cope in the severe winters of 1947 and 1963? It's a mystery to me!

Snowmaggedon

It's all over the internet, it's been on the
front page
Forget your global warming, they've
declared a new ice age
A national disaster – we're all on the
slippery slope
They say it's 'snowmaggedon' and we
really just can't cope!

The snowflake generation cannot make it
into school
'The playground is too icy' states a health
and safety rule
The trains have all been cancelled, it was
on the radio
Oh silly me the reason is of course
'wrong type of snow'

The word down at the Co-op is there's
been a massive panic
They're emptying the shelves of food –
the housewives, they're all manic
They rush down to the shops when they
detect the slightest flurry
Then post a photo of the snow on
Facebook in a hurry

(Cont...)

I wish these namby pamby folk would
stop their constant bleating
'Cos we're the generation who did not
have central heating
Inside our bedroom windows there was
ice upon the glass
We'd huddle round the coal fire trying to
warm our frozen ass

We just pulled on our wellies and then
off to school we went
Even in that winter they defined as
'discontent'
We made a giant ice slide and we played
on it with glee
We thought we had it good we'd never
heard of S.A.D.

But nowadays in winter they all tend to
get the jitters
As soon as there's a flake of snow they're
calling out the gritters
At last the snow is melting but it isn't
looking good
I've just heard on the news that they
predict a bloomin' flood!

A Teenage Dream

I was lucky enough to be a teenager in the 1970s. They say times were simpler then but there was nothing simple about taping the top 40 on the radio on a cassette player and trying to curl your hair with antiquated curling tongs, especially during a power cut. Sit back and enjoy a trip down memory lane to what, in my opinion, was the most iconic decade of the 20th Century – the 1970s.

A Teenage Dream

'The times they are a changing', and
blimey that's the truth
'Cos things ain't like they used to be
when I was in my youth
It may be over forty years since I became
a teen
I couldn't wait for Thursday for my *Jackie*
magazine

Turning to the problem page we read
Cathy and Claire
Letters about teenage angst and tales of
deep despair
They told us how to kiss, we had to
practise on our hand
But petting in the swimming baths was
definitely banned

If a lad was keen he'd send a message
through your mate
Or pass a note under the desk to ask you
for a date
No Tinder and no Instagram, no
Snapchat and no apps
It seems they're sending 'cock shots' now
those bold pubescent chaps

(Cont...)

Mascara came in shades of blue we
followed all the trends
But how come kids today don't seem to
suffer from split ends?
Charlie perfume for the girls and *Old Spice*
for the lads
They didn't need to buy it they just
pinched it from their dads

We met our mates in Woolworths by the
famous *Pick and Mix*
We didn't need to use fake tan in 1976
We couldn't wait to get outdoors and soak
up UV rays
Baby Oil was sunscreen way back in those
halcyon days

Findus Crispy Pancakes on a Friday was a
treat
Finished off with *Arctic Roll*, we always
had a sweet
We had to share it round we only had a
tiny piece
A tin of peas was junk food so we didn't
get obese

We learned to jazz our jeans up with a
piece of fancy braid
And went to the school disco in a dress
our mothers made
In Needlework at school we learned to
make a lovely smock
And for a treat from *Chelsea Girl* we
bought a special frock

(Cont...)

Freeman Hardy Willis sold a range of
platform shoes
And only cons and servicemen were
covered in tattoos
You won't believe the latest trend they're
wearing those ripped jeans
We sewed on fancy patches back when we
were in our teens

Teens today make fun of us but well they
shouldn't laugh
'Cos Ugg boots are like slippers and their
Crocs are pretty naff
Why do they all wear camouflage? I find
it rather odd
They're hiding from their enemies, the
cyber bully squad

The world is changing quickly and we're
trying to keep up
It's pretty hard competing with a vigorous
young pup
They're wanting to replace us with a
juvenile high flyer
But now they've changed the rules and so
we can't bloomin' retire!

Back to the Eighties

*Well after writing a homage to the 1970s,
I felt I should follow that up with a poem
about the 1980s. This was the decade that I
started work, got married, bought a house
and even managed to move up the property
ladder a couple of times. How times have
changed! A completely different mood to
the seventies poem but then they were very
different decades...*

Back to the Eighties

In the eighties greed was good
We'd Lady Di and Zola Budd
The city rose, the unions fell
Brixton riots and poll tax hell

The 1980s – big and brash
'Loadsa money' instant cash
Giant phones with battery packs
Yuppies with their filofax

Pop stars wearing Ray Ban shades
Terrified they'd die of AIDS
Ageing actor in the White House
Yorkshire Ripper in the court house

They tore down the Berlin Wall
'Free Mandela' was the call
On Page Three Samantha Fox
While famine rages, Live Aid rocks

The Falklands War was Maggie's glory
The Miners' Strike another story
British Gas – now place your bid
Buy some shares and just 'Ask Sid'

Council houses at half price
New stone cladding – very nice
Now you're posh you feel much better
Eating prawns and Viennetta

(Cont...)

Ra-ra skirts and shoulder pads
Stonewashed denims for the lads
Wearing shell suits, very brave
Mullet hair, the permanent wave

Watching *Dallas* on TV
Miami Vice and *Dynasty*
New romantics, MTV
Microchip technology

No Instagram and no You Tube
A skateboard or a Rubik's Cube
A Care Bear or a BMX
Instead of Google – Teletext

Thatcher's children came of age
Worked hard to earn a decent wage
They're paying off their student debt
They can't afford a mortgage yet!

The Rhyme of My Life: The story of Mrs Yorkshire the Baking Bard

Night Mail poem

So when did all this 'poetry malarkey' begin? Well, when I was in the second year of high school we read a poem by W H Auden, *Night Mail*. You may be familiar with the poem.

At the time there were problems with the roof of our high school so the first and second year pupils were re-located to a disused Victorian school near the city centre. The classrooms had large windows which were located above head height, preventing children from daydreaming out of the window or being distracted by the world outside. It was a late afternoon lesson and by now my thoughts were turning to catching the bus home with friends. Beams of sun boldly

Ings Road School, Wakefield

streamed into the room and I watched the dust particles dancing within them, willing the time to pass.

Our English teacher began reading the poem and suddenly I was transfixed. The rhythm of the poem conjured up the image of the train bustling through the British night-time countryside. I wanted

92

to be able to write poetry like that. I'd read books and pieces of prose but this was something else. This was like dancing instead of walking.

The ability to connect with someone, anyone, whether friends or strangers, through the power of words, both fascinated and thrilled me in equal measure.

In that moment I realised that through the use of language in all its beauty and different forms, I could reach into the hearts and minds of people and make them laugh, cry, contemplate, examine, reflect and ultimately share my passion for the words and their message.

Our homework was set – to write a poem in the same style. A train journey, any train journey of our choice. I could see my classmates were packing their books away. To them it was just the end of another boring lesson. I felt detached from my surroundings. My mind was racing. I was already thinking about what I was going to write.

I queued up for the school bus. I was the chatterbox of the group and often led the conversation which usually revolved around pop music, fashion, a TV programme or techniques implemented to achieve the latest hairstyle, but I was still distracted. Words and rhymes were already running around my head in anticipation of writing my poem.

I ran into the house and as usual we gathered round the table for our tea. It was a busy, noisy house. Four children and two adults. There was always plenty of activity. People coming and going. The constant clatter of pots and pans from the kitchen. Radio Eireann blasting out Irish music, my mum singing along and my father occasionally playing his tin whistle. There were the usual altercations, raised voices and doors slamming.

I shared a bedroom with my older sister but fortunately this evening she was otherwise engaged watching TV downstairs, which was just as well because there was an unwritten rule that being the oldest she was in charge. It was primarily her bedroom. Most evenings the whole family would huddle round the fire in the living room to watch TV as there was no central heating in the house. Some evenings I braved the cold in my bedroom to listen to Radio Luxembourg on a transistor radio, a pop music station which broadcasted on 208 medium wave every evening during the 1970s. The DJ, Tony Prince, or my favourite, 'Kid' Jensen, would host *The Battle of the Bands* – the *Bay City Rollers vs The Osmonds* or *David Cassidy vs David Essex*. My sister sometimes listened with me.

If I had enough pocket money I'd buy the *Fabulous 208* magazine which listed the song lyrics of all my favourite artists of the day. I'd carefully remove the staples from the centre pages and place the full colour poster spread across the middle pages on the wall above my bed.

I relished the fact that I had the bedroom to myself and wasted no time in retrieving my English homework book from my school bag which I'd thrown hastily on the bed. I had to kneel on the floor against the bed, my legs tucked underneath me, using the bed as a makeshift desk. The candlewick bedspread against my body and legs kept me warm and I'd closed the door to block out the noise from the rest of the family downstairs. I remembered the poem by Auden. As the teacher read it aloud I'd heard the underlying rhythm, mimicking the sound of a train on the tracks.

I began writing and found the ability to use the correct amount of stressed and unstressed syllables in each line came easily to me, as though I was singing a song. Once I started writing it was a like a tap had been turned on in my head. The words came flowing out, spilling onto the page. An exhilarating journey of creativity and self-discovery.

I was pleased with my efforts and duly handed my homework in. A couple of days later at the beginning of the lesson the English teacher moved around the room, skilfully dodging the school bags carelessly discarded on the floor, as if negotiating an army assault course. He shouted out each pupil's mark as he handed back their homework. Sometimes he paused and made comments: 'good effort', 'watch your spelling'. I waited impatiently for my homework to be returned until he only had one book left in his hand.

As he returned to his desk a wave of panic rose within me. Had I misunderstood the instructions and written something completely different to everyone else? A sudden rush of heat enveloped me and I sat up straight in my chair, arms folded in front of me as if to protect myself from the inevitable onslaught of humiliation and mortification.

After what seemed like an age he held my book up and proceeded to inform the class that he wanted to read my poem to everyone as an example of the correct interpretation of the homework set! He was very impressed by my use of metre and rhyme. He told the class to listen to the rhythm as he read.

My face still burned like a hot pan on a stove, the anticipation of hearing my poem read aloud bubbling inside me. An extraordinary sense of elation swept over me as I listened to him read the poem, just as I'd intended it to be read. I could hear the rhythm of the train – my train, not the train with the *Night Mail,* but the one I'd envisaged rattling along the tracks through verdant countryside on a warm summer's day.

I felt dizzy with delight. I wanted to close my eyes and savour the moment. All eyes were upon me. There were audible gasps and murmurs of appreciation.The ball in my throat threatened to escape my lips. I burned with a fierce joy.

That was just the beginning of my love affair with language and words. Whenever the teacher asked us to write a story for homework, I became completely engrossed. Nothing else was important. During the subsequent lessons I became distracted. My mind was like a butterfly fluttering back to the story I'd already started writing in my head.

By the time I reached the fourth year I had a different but no less encouraging English teacher. His name was Mr Devlin. He always read my stories to the class. I think he appreciated my enthusiasm, even though I was a 'lively' member of the class, partial to a fair amount of giggling and chattering.

Age 16, centre of photo

One day, as we were filing past his desk to go to the next lesson, he stopped me and told me I had a gift and I musn't waste it. A gift? What did that mean to a 15-year-

St Thomas à Becket School.

old girl, and what did he mean that I musn't waste it? OK so I could write a good story, tell a good tale, but I put that down to my Irish upbringing. I was from a working class family and shouldn't get ideas above my station. I'd leave school, maybe go to college, get a job, meet a nice young man, get married and start a family.

And that's exactly what I did. I left school, went to secretarial college, got a job, met a nice young man, got married and had a daughter. I still read books when I had the time. Occasionally, if someone was leaving work or having a special birthday, I wrote a poem. I didn't even bother to keep copies.

Once I became a mother it was all-consuming. I wanted to recreate *The Little House on the Prairie*. To be the perfect wife and mother. To indulge my child with my time and make her childhood as magical as possible. To be an accomplished housekeeper and cook. 'She always keeps a good table'. That's what I used to hear when I was growing up.

Eventually my husband, Michael and I,

together with our daughter, Jessica, re-located from Yorkshire to live on the Isle of Man.

Maughold Village, Isle of Man

A couple of years later Jessica went across the sea to Queen's University in Belfast and suddenly there was just the two of us. I was in my late forties. She left university, got a job and settled in the north of Ireland. We had an empty nest and our thoughts turned to slowing down and not working so many hours.

We were running our small mail order company together when my husband returned to working in advertising. We scaled the mail order company down and essentially I was working part time.

At the top of Maughold Head

I missed my daughter terribly and felt it would be a good distraction to indulge myself a little. I started walking for pleasure and fitness. I baked cakes for friends and family. Whatever the occasion I'd turn up with a cake!

I was sitting down one day, my thoughts turning to life on the Isle of Man and all its quirks and curiosities. We would have been living here nine years in just over a month. I started to write, not with

Selling my cupcakes

99

a pen but with a keyboard. My fingers danced skilfully across the keys as ideas popped into my head. It was like an epiphany, I could write a poem to celebrate because I could write poetry! Of course I could write poetry, I used to write poetry, why hadn't I written poetry for so long?

I read the poem to my husband. He thought it was very good. Would he have dared tell me if it was rubbish? I wasn't too sure. My friend Sonia came round. She's a straight talking Geordie lass. Kind but honest. She listened intently and when I'd finished she said it was brilliant. She encouraged me to post it on Facebook.

I still wasn't convinced and read it to a couple of other people who were similarly impressed. Sonia beseeched me to post the poem on Facebook so that others could enjoy and appreciate it, particularly our friends on the island. After much deliberation, a month later, on the ninth anniversary of moving here, I took the plunge and posted the poem on my Facebook page.

I was like that 13-year-old girl again, filled with uncertainty and anticipation. However, within minutes the poem was being commented on favourably and shared all over Facebook. Of course, I still doubted myself: after all, these were my friends. They wouldn't be cruel enough to criticise the composition I'd carefully created and crafted for their enjoyment. I wrote a couple more poems and these too were received very positively.

A few months later I joined the Isle of Man Poetry Society. I hadn't even realised there was one except a friend told me about it. I went along to the meeting with only three poems in my folder.

A group of people were sitting around a large table. Each member read a poem to the group, either one that they'd written or one from a book. I began to think I'd probably made a mistake as the poetry didn't appear to be in the same vein as mine. Oh dear, what would they make of my poetry? There was to be a break for coffee half-way through and I considered leaving quietly through the back door.

Just before we broke for coffee a gentleman began reading one of his own compositions. As he began reading I felt relief wash over me. His poetry was a very similar style to mine.

The chairperson asked if I had anything I'd like to read so I nervously retrieved my poem about the Isle of Man from my folder and began to read. It's a humorous and affectionate poem entitled *The Come Over*.

They appeared to be laughing in all the correct places. I finished and held my breath. Everyone clapped. Thank goodness – I hadn't offended anyone and they actually appeared to enjoy my poetry.

We had coffee and I chatted to the gentleman who read before me. He was there with his wife, also a talented poet.

It transpired that he was something of a local celebrity. He wrote a column in the Manx Independent, the island's main newspaper, and featured on local radio once a week. Indeed, much like Cher, Cilla and Lulu, he was known by only one name: 'Pullyman'. I felt I was in the presence of some rather special people.

In the second half of the meeting another gentleman began reading his own poetry. This blew my mind. He appeared to have an encyclopaedic knowledge of rhyming and metre schemes and this was reflected in his poetry which was both witty and superbly written.

After the meeting the gentleman, whose name is Dennis Turner, approached me and asked if he could discuss my poetry with me as he enjoyed it very much. His words were 'I think you've got something'.

I met with Dennis and we chatted over my homemade cake and a cup of Yorkshire Tea. He spoke to me about my use of 'feminine endings'. I didn't even know there was such a thing but apparently I was using these to great effect!

I felt honoured that he was imparting his knowledge to me. He said he couldn't really teach me anything as I instinctively followed the rules of good metre and rhyme but he wanted me to know why I was doing what I did.

I was like a child, hungry for knowledge and eager to learn. He began talking about iambic, trochaic, spondaic and dactylic metres. He explained the use of stressed and unstressed syllables. I vaguely remembered some of it from school. Poetry became increasingly fascinating.

I know his in-depth knowledge of metre and rhyme which he has so generously shared with me and continues to do so, inspires me to this day and has improved my writing beyond measure.

Performing with IOM poets

Through the Poetry Society meetings I discovered the poetry Open Mic events which take place on the island. These are organised by another very talented poet called Hazel Teare. Hazel also comperes these evenings.

I'd enjoyed amateur dramatics at school and quite often took the lead role in school productions. Maybe this was because I had a loud voice, but either way I figured this would come in handy at the Open Mic events and for performing in public!

Performing as a witch, age 15

The Open Mic events have grown in such popularity that spectators are regularly turned away as they're full to capacity. They've also given me the opportunity to hone my performance skills considerably.

Performing at Manx Litfest

Hazel started the Open Mic evenings a few years before to give anyone wishing to perform their poetry a platform. It was a kind of rebellion against the stuffy academic image poetry has and the idea that only academics can successfully produce good poetry. Making poetry accessible to all is the key to their success.

Performing at the Isle of Man Hospice 35th Anniversary event for volunteers, Douglas

Once I became involved with the poetry scene on the island I soon began performing at local charity events and private functions. I tailor my poetry to suit the audience and find the more I perform the easier it becomes.

I decided to create a public Facebook page to share my poetry and that's when I came up with the idea for a pen name. Since living on the island I've become known as *Mrs Yorkshire* as I'm instantly recognisable by my accent. I'm also well-known for my baking skills so I put the two together and came up with *Mrs Yorkshire the Baking Bard.*

The page enabled me to connect with poetry lovers from all over the world. As I write observational poetry on all subjects, I've been able to share poems of specific interest to certain groups and attract more followers.

On special occasions I share relevant poetry. At Christmas I share my poem *Carol for Christmas*. On Valentine's Day I share my poem *A Yorkshire Valentine* and, of course, I always share my *Halloween* poem on 31st October. During the year there are many other special days such as St Patrick's Day, Yorkshire Day, Breast Cancer Awareness month – the list is endless.

Facebook: Mrs Yorkshire the Baking Bard

I also began writing poetry with certain days in mind. On National Poetry Day a couple of years ago I wrote a poem and posted it to Channel 5's daytime TV show *The Wright Stuff*. I was stunned when they actually read it out live on air.

I wrote a poem to celebrate International Women's Day and this time Matthew Wright, the presenter of the show, contacted me and asked me if I'd like to video the poem so that I could read it myself on the show! I was absolutely delighted and duly did so.

The Wright Stuff

A few months later it was announced he was leaving the show after eighteen years.

I was so grateful for his kindness that I sent him good wishes and wrote a few lines in verse to wish him well.

The Wright Stuff

Matthew contacted me again and asked if I'd be kind enough to video the poem to feature on his final show. I was honoured and delighted to do this. I've since appeared on *The Jeremy Vine Show,* which replaced *The Wright Stuff,* reading a poem for National Poetry Day again.

I've also had my poems published in many local and national newspapers and magazines.

My husband, Michael, convinced me that I should set up a Youtube channel so I've made videos of a few of my poems and uploaded them onto there too. Go to youtube.com and type in 'Mrs Yorkshire' to view the videos on my channel.

During this time a very good friend of ours came to visit us on the island. Chris Payne is a very successful and highly respected businessman who began his career in marketing in the 1980s. He has worked as a reviews editor, mainly for computer magazines, and created Europe's largest mail order supplier of light and sound machines including lucid dreaming machines and other devices. He's currently the Managing Director of Effort-Free

Media Ltd, helping consultants, trainers and coaches to create quality e-products they can give away and sell.

Chris had been reading my poetry online and watching my videos on my Youtube channel. He encouraged me to publish my poetry. I told him it was a dream of mine to publish a book and he convinced me that, with his help, it would happen. He advised me to write a trilogy of books, each of the three books on a different theme, and suggested that each poem should have an illustration to accompany it.

I was lucky enough to find a very talented, experienced and highly respected artist and illustrator, Graeme Hogg at *The Whole Hogg*. His illustrations have brought my poetry to life. I never even considered illustrating the books but I'm so pleased I did. You can have a look at more of Graeme's work on his web site https://thewholehogg.carbonmade.com/. You won't be disappointed.

So, after not even three years of re-discovering my love of poetry, here I am publishing a trilogy of poetry books. I'm 56 years old and have realised it's never too late to follow your dreams and make them come true. I've had a lot of support and encouragement and made lots of friends along the way.

My books are available to purchase

separately or as a trilogy at a reduced price. If you've purchased any of my books from Amazon, please leave me feedback in the reviews. It's great to connect with my readers.

I'm always open to requests to write on any subject, so if you think there's something I should write about, drop me a line and tell me!

You can write to me at c/o Red Lizard Ltd, PO Box 18, Ramsey, Isle of Man, British Isles, IM99 4PG, e-mail me at carolellis2012@gmail.com, or message me through my Facebook page: *Mrs Yorkshire the Baking Bard.*

I'm happy to post signed copies of books. I accept commissions to write poetry to order. If you have a specific event or celebration, as long as I have a few details regarding the person you'd like the poem for, I can come up with something especially for them. I'm also happy to perform at corporate and charity events, social functions and engage in TV and radio appearances.

I have a book stuffed full of ideas for poems, all waiting to be written. If there were more hours in the day I could fill them writing poetry. I know I'll never run out of things to write about if I live to be over 100 years old!

Thank you for reading my poetry. My original dream as a 13-year-old girl was to share my love of words with the world and, finally, I believe that dream has come true.

Carol Ellis
Mrs Yorkshire the Baking Bard
X

Also available

Also available

Mrs Yorkshire the Baking Bard
c/o Red Lizard Ltd
PO Box 18
Ramsey
Isle of Man
IM99 4PG

carolellis2012@gmail.com

Facebook: Mrs Yorkshire the Baking Bard

YouTube: Mrs Yorkshire

Give it a Go

Why not have a go at writing your own poetry? I believe you can write a poem about any subject. Write down a few ideas about what you'd like to say about your subject matter and let each idea form a verse.

If you're stuck for a rhyme, use the *Rhymezone* web site, it's far more useful than going through the alphabet in your head, chanting rhyming words!

As you've probably gathered, I like to write rhyming poetry with good, structured metre. Metre is the basic rhythmic structure of a verse or lines in a poem. I find poetry with structured metre much easier to recite and much easier for the reader to read too. If you're in doubt about whether a line 'scans', even after you've read it back, count the number of syllables in each line to see if they match. You may need to swap one word for another so that it fits. A Thesaurus is very useful for this. There is a web site called *Thesaurus* to make it even easier for you.

I've left a few blank pages at the back of this book for you to write down your ideas and, who knows, you may release your inner poet. Go on, give it a go. You may find you enjoy writing poetry as

much as reading it. Why not write
a poem about something we can all
relate to? You can make it humorous,
sentimental, thought-provoking – the
possibilities are endless. Overleaf I've
written the first couple of lines of a
poem to start you off. Keep your verses
to four lines each in rhyming couplets.
Good luck!

Mrs Yorkshire the Baking Bard x

Here are the first two lines of a poem to inspire you to write the rest. Good luck!

Pay Day

When I awoke one day last week I found
to my dismay
Already I was skint and it
was two weeks to pay day